BY DEREK TAYLOR KENT
ILLUSTRATED BY BRIGHT JUNGLE STUDIOS

DINOSAURS LOVE CHASING.

2

DINOS COME FROM FAR OFF PLACES,
ENGINES READY, JUST FOR RACES.

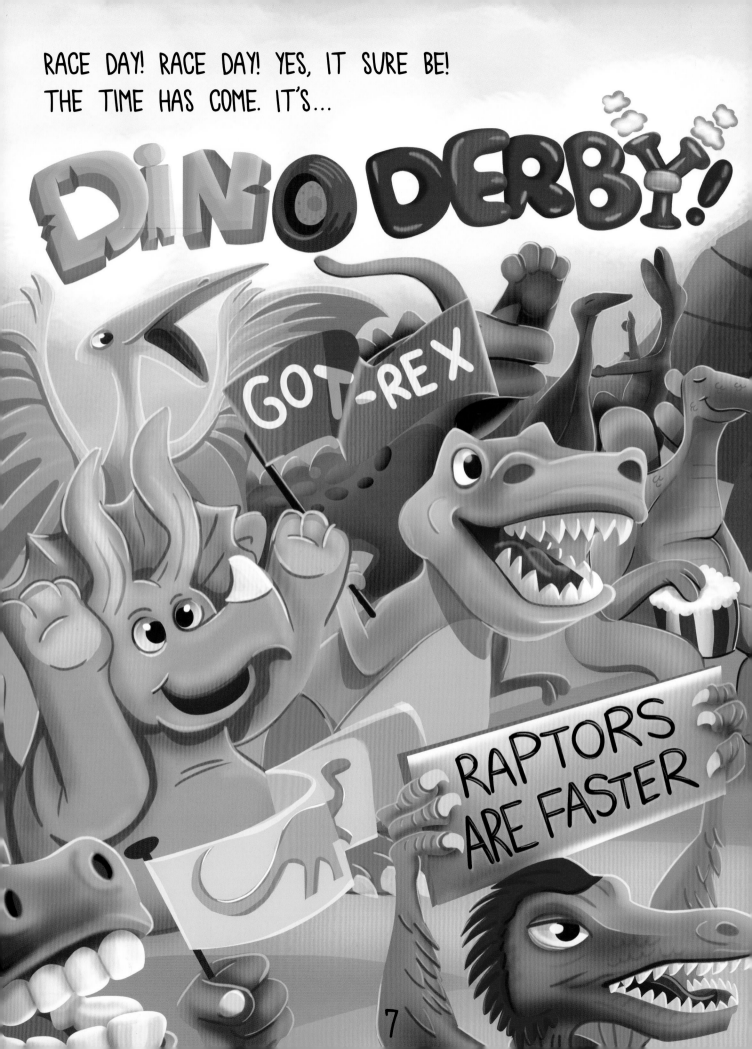

"YOU TINY DINOS HAVE NO CHANCE!"
LAUGH GIANT DINOS AT FIRST GLANCE.
"DON'T GET CLOSE OR TAKE MY SEAT
OR YOU'LL GET CRUSHED BENEATH MY FEET!"

WHO TAKES THE LEAD ON TOUGH TERRAIN?
TRICERATOPS THAT'S IN A TRAIN!
IT HAS THREE HORNS AND BEEPS THEM LOUD,
BUT WILL IT WIN AND BEAT THE CROWD?

FROM BEHIND, HERE COMES A SUITOR...
STEGOSAURUS ON A SCOOTER!
WITH SPIKY TAIL AND PLATED BACK
IT WHIPS THE WIND, DEFLECTS ATTACK!

WHO'S THAT DIVING THROUGH THE RAIN?
IT'S DIPLODOCUS IN A PLANE!
HOW DOES SHE FIT INSIDE THAT PIT?
SHE SAYS, "IT'S SIMPLE. I JUST SIT!"

SOME MAY FLY, BUT OTHERS FLOAT,
LIKE SPINOSAURUS IN A BOAT.
ENGINE'S OUT? NO NEED TO BAIL,
JUST USE YOUR BACKBONE AS A SAIL!

SOMETHING BURST OUT FROM THE FOREST...
IT'S ARMORED DINO - ANKYLOSAURUS!
HOW DOES IT MOVE WITH HEAVY PLATES?
IT SINGS, "I GROOVE ON ROLLER SKATES!"

14

GALLIMIMUS IN A CHOPPER!

HADROSAURUS ON A HOPPER!

15

PTEROSAURS IN
BIG BALLOON!

IGUANADON IN OLD PONTOON!

16

THE FINISH LINE IS NOT TOO FAR,
BUT HERE COMES T-REX IN A CAR!
SHE ROARS, "YOU BEST NOT PLACE BEFORE US!
I'M THE GREAT TYRANNOSAURUS!"

THE TIRE POPS! WILL IT IMPACT HER?
SHE SPOTS A FAST VELOCIRAPTOR.

SHE LEAPS ONTO THE RAPTOR'S TRACTOR,
AND TAKES THE RAPTOR AS HER CAPTOR!

18

THAT'S TOO MUCH WEIGHT. IT LOSES SPEED,
SO TINY DINOS TAKE THE LEAD!

19

A MICRORAPTOR AND DILONG
ARE FLYING FAST AND RUNNING STRONG!

20

THE FINISH LINE IS THERE TO SEE.
A PHOTO FINISH IT MAY BE!
LEGS ARE DASHING, TEETH ARE GNASHING,
HORNS ARE MASHING, ALL GO CRASHING!

21

WOW, THAT RACE WAS MIGHTY FUN.
LET'S LOOK CLOSE AND SEE WHO WON.

THE TINY DINOS WON THIS DAY!
EVERY DINO SHOUTS, "HOORAY!"
RAISE YOUR TROPHY FOR FIRST PLACE,
FOR ANY SIZE CAN WIN THE RACE.

24

THANKS FOR READING DINOSAUR DERBY!
WANT TO LEARN MORE ABOUT THE DINOS IN THE RACE?

1. TYRANNOSAURUS REX
2. VELOCIRAPTOR
3. STEGOSAURUS
4. TRICERATOPS
5. DIPLODOCUS
6. DILONG
7. MICRORAPTOR

8. GALLIMIMUS
9. IGUANADON
10. HADROSAUR

11. PTEROSAUR
12. SPINOSAURUS
13. ANKYLOSAURUS

Whimsical World

Books by Derek Taylor Kent:

Simon and the Solar System (ages 4-9)	*Counting Sea Life with the Little Seahorse (ages 2-4)*
El Perro con Sombrero (ages 3-8)	*Principal Mikey (ages 7-12)*
El Perro con Sombrero meets	*Rudy and the Beast:*
Los Gatos con Gelatos (ages 3-8)	*My Homework Ate My Dog! (ages 9-12)*
Doggy Claus/Perro Noel (ages 3-8)	*Kubrick's Game (ages 13+)*
The Scary School series (ages 7-12, 4-book series)	*The Grossest Picture Book Ever (ages 3-9)*

www.WhimsicalWorldBooks.com
www.DerekTaylorKent.com

Library of Congress Cataloging-in-Publication Data
Kent, Derek Taylor
Dinosaur Derby / Derek Taylor Kent : Illustrations by Bright Jungle Studios,
Filip Trajkovski, Loreta Stefanovska, Angela Koneska, Risto Manasiev
28 pages 8,5 x 11,0 in
ISBN: 978-1-949213-07-2
For information on bulk purchases, please contact Whimsical World sales department at
info@WhimsicalWorldBooks.com

First Edition—2020 / Designed by Bright Jungle Studios
Printed in China